nickelodeon

TIME TO BE KIND!

 S0-BZE-438

By Annie Cooke

Illustrated by **Benjamin Burch**

A GOLDEN BOOK · NEW YORK

T#: 688746
rhcbooks.com
ISBN 978-0-593-12394-2
Printed in the United States of America
10 9 8 7 6 5 4 3 2 1

Corn and Peg were up early, ready for another do-gooding day! They couldn't wait to read their new Captain Thunderhoof comic book.

After they'd finished the whole exciting story, Peg began to read the do-gooder pledge: "'I am a do-gooder—that's guaranteed. . . .'"

"'Whenever I can, I do a good deed!'" Corn finished.
"Captain Thunderhoof is amazing," said Peg, "because
she always makes time to be kind."

"We always make time to be kind. I guess that makes us *kind* of amazing, too!" Corn joked.

"Good one, Corn," Peg laughed. "But the truth is, whenever we lend a helping hoof, we're being kind."

"And we're kind to every pony in Galloping Grove!" Corn added.

"We were kind when we invited Ferris to join Carrot Club, because it's kind to make everyone feel included," Corn said.

"And," said Peg, "when we helped Sheriff Swiftstone direct traffic. He was busy, and it was kind to help him!"

"And when we returned that runaway ball to its owner, that was being kind, too," Corn said excitedly. "Being kind—and doing good—is what we do!" Peg cheered.

"When we helped Mail Carrier Pintock deliver her mail in the snow," said Corn,

"and then fixed her torn bag, that was *two* acts of kindness!"
"Double the kindness, double the smiles!" laughed Peg.

"Kindness also means doing the right thing
even when it's hard," said Peg.

"It sure does!" agreed Corn. "Like when Mayor Montagu
needed help carrying all those boxes to his car, we helped—
even though that meant we missed out on the Captain
Thunderhoof stickers at the comics shop. That *was* hard, but
it was also super kind!"

"It's like Captain Thunderhoof says—being kind makes you feel *thunder*-rific!" Corn said.

"Being kind can make our friends feel *thunder*-rific, too,"
said Peg. "Like when we were kind to Paolo and it gave
him the confidence to perform in the talent show."

"We always make time to be kind, just like Captain Thunderhoof!" Corn exclaimed.

Just then, Corn and Peg heard a cry for help from Ferdy. His balloon had blown away in the wind!

"Don't worry, Ferdy!" Corn shouted as the pair rushed to him and his brother, Ferris.

"Uh-oh. Ferdy looks like he's about to fall,"
said Peg, worried.

"I've got him!" Corn said. He reached Ferris
just as Ferdy wobbled sideways. Corn caught
him and placing him safely on the ground.

Meanwhile, Peg flew up to the balloon as fast as she could. Stretching, she caught the string and landed gracefully beside Corn.

Peg handed the balloon to Corn.
"To make sure it doesn't get away again,
I'll tie the string around your hoof!" Corn said.

"Thanks, Corn and Peg!" Ferdy said.
"You're welcome, Ferdy," said Peg.
"We can *always* make time to be kind!"